Richard Scarry's
NiCKY GOES TO THE DOCTOR

written and illustrated by Richard Scarry

A Random House PICTUREBACK® Book

RANDOM HOUSE 🏠 NEW YORK

Copyright © 1972, 1978 by Richard Scarry. All rights reserved. This 2014 edition was published in the United States by Random House Children's Books, a division of Random House LLC, a Penguin Random House Company, 1745 Broadway, New York, NY 10019, and in Canada by Random House of Canada Limited, Toronto. Originally published in a slightly different form by Golden Books, an imprint of Random House Children's Books, New York, in 1972. Pictureback, Random House, and the Random House colophon are registered trademarks of Random House LLC.
Library of Congress Control Number: 76-187503
ISBN: 978-0-307-11842-4
Visit us on the Web! randomhouse.com/kids
Educators and librarians, for a variety of teaching tools, visit us at RHTeachersLibrarians.com
Printed in the United States of America
10 9 8 7 6 5 4 3
Random House Children's Books supports the First Amendment and celebrates the right to read.

Nicky Bunny was going to the doctor.
He waved to all his friends as he and
his mother drove through town.
"I'm going to see the doctor,"
he shouted.

AUTO TRANSPORTER

POLICE

Nurse Nightingale met them at the door. "It's so nice to see you," she said. "Won't you please come in?"

While Nicky was waiting for the doctor, Nurse Nightingale showed him a book. It told him the right things to eat to help him grow big and strong.

Then it was time to see Dr. Doctor.

"Hello, Doctor," said Nicky.

"Hello, young fellow," said Dr. Doctor. "Please take off your shirt and slacks so I can examine you."

"My, how you've grown since you were here last," said the doctor. "Even your ears."

"You've gained weight, too," said Dr. Doctor.
"That's because I always eat everything
Mommy gives me," said Nicky.

Nicky had to laugh when the doctor examined his stomach. "Excuse me, Doctor," said Nicky, "I'm ticklish."

"Perfectly normal," said Dr. Doctor.

"Now say 'A-a-ah,'" said the doctor.
"A-a-ah!" said Nicky, and the doctor looked
down his throat.

The doctor looked at Nicky's ears. He took a
long look, because Nicky had long ears.

The doctor put his stethoscope on Nicky's back, to listen to him breathing. Whish-whoosh, whish-whoosh, the air went in and out of Nicky's lungs.

Then the doctor put his stethoscope on Nicky's chest. Thump-thump, thump-thump went Nicky's heart.

"Listen to my heart," said Dr. Doctor.
And Nicky heard the doctor's heart go
thump-thump, thump-thump.

The doctor tapped Nicky's knee with a little hammer, and Nicky's foot jumped up by itself. "That's a very fine knee you have, Nicky," said Dr. Doctor.

Then Dr. Doctor gave Nicky a shot.
"Ouch!" said Nicky. "I don't like shots."
"Nobody likes shots," said the doctor, "but we need them sometimes to help us stay healthy and well."
"I know," said Nicky.

"Now we'll test your eyes,"
said the doctor. He showed Nicky
some pictures.

"I see a carrot, a pear, a
strawberry, a banana, and a
blueberry," said Nicky. "I like
the carrot the best."

"You have good, sharp eyes,"
said Dr. Doctor.

"Well, Nicky," said Dr. Doctor, "you're healthy and growing nicely. Get dressed and Nurse Nightingale will give you a balloon."

"Thank you, Doctor," said Nicky.

At home, Mrs. Bunny told Mr. Bunny how much Nicky had grown. "Just keep it up," said Mr. Bunny proudly to Nicky. "Some day you'll be as tall as I am!"

Then Nicky told his brothers and sisters all about his visit to the doctor. And they all wanted to go, too.

"Be patient," said Mrs. Bunny. "I can't take you all at once. You'll have to take turns."

The children were patient. They all finally did visit the doctor, and he found them all healthy and well.

Wasn't that nice?